WHEN LIONS COULD FLY

BY

JAMAL KORAM

SEA ISLAND INFORMATION GROUP
BELTSVILLE, MARYLAND 20705

When Lions Could Fly
African Lion Tales
ISBN 1-877610-01-1

Copyright, 1989, Jamal Koram
This book may not be reproduced in any manner without permission from the author.

All Rights Reserved
Second Edition
Second Printing

Cover Design by Jamal Koram

Illustrations by Marcy Dunn Ramsey
Cover Illustrated by Marcy Dunn Ramsey

When Lions Could Fly is available on audio cassette

Manufactured in the United States of America

To order additional copies, write or call:

Sea Island Information Group
P.O. Box 10628
Silver Spring, Md 20914 USA
(301) 937-2494

DEDICATED TO

Modupe Ogunkeye Clarke
"May peace be upon her always.
May her spirit be forever with us."

and for my children:
Anika, Nilaja, Khente, and Omari

and for my god-children:
Donyelle, Khristia, Kyle Rashid, Shelitria,
and Keisha

and for my nieces and nephews:
Imani, Tahir, Imani, Heather, Kristina, Mathew, Ryan,
Derrick, Dennis, David, Sean, Dwayne, Allease
Vincent, Desiree, Bradley, Lance

and those of my extended families:
Ayodele

and for the children of
Greenburgh
White Plains
Poughkeepsie
Catonsville
Charlottesville
Baltimore

and for
Our Children Everywhere

"Peace, Love, and Respect for Everyone!"

iii

About the Author

Jamal Koram is a storyteller, poet, educational consultant, cultural advocate, businessman, and father. He was born in Greenburgh, New York and currently resides in Maryland.

As a storyteller, Mr. Koram has performed in schools, colleges and universities, libraries, festivals, and on T.V. and radio. He is a member of the Association of Black Storytellers, and currently serves on that Board of Directors (1989).

His performance is called "Kenyatta's Afro Tales with Jamal Koram the StoryMan."

"Sifa Zote Ziende Kwa Watoto Ulimwengu"

"Sifa Zote Ziende Kwa Watoto Afrika"

"Sifa Zote Ziende Kwa Muuamba"

(All praises to the children of the world; All praises to the children of Africa; All praises to the Creator) Peace.

TABLE OF CONTENTS

INTRODUCTION

In African traditions, the Lion is a symbol of power and royalty, however, in some African tales the Lion is often on the losing end of many circumstances, as the weaker animals find ways of outwitting the stronger, more powerful Lion. Not so, with this collection.

In WHEN LIONS COULD FLY, the Lion is loyal, wise, generous, and sometimes devious. But, no matter what role the Lion, or Lioness, is playing he/she will always take a stand based on positive principles. These stories are for all ages. Children will respond to the reading of these Lion Tales if they are read with gusto. Change your voice levels, act out the different parts in a story, assume different voices for the different actors in a story. I hope that they will bring you enjoyment and knowledge. Maybe we will see each other soon. Until then, keep me in your prayers.

Peace and Love

Jamal Koram the StoryMan

WHEN LION'S COULD FLY

"Storyteller!"

"Yes, my son."

"Is it true that the Lion is the King of the forest?"

"Yes my son."

"If it is true, Storyteller, then why is it that when a Lion is hunted, the Lion always loses?"

"It will be that way, my son, until the Lion tells the story."

Brothe
Tejumol

HOW THE LION GOT HIS ROAR
Adapted by Jamal Koram the StoryMan
A West African Tale

he Lion did not always have a powerful voice.
t one time the Lion had a little mew-mew voice,
ke a kitty cat.

)ne day the hare came to the Lion. He said,
Master Lion, I hate to tell you this, but I must
ell you. All of the other animals are laughing
ehind your back. They are laughing at your
ittle mew-mew voice."

he Lion had a big frown on his face, and in a
oice like a little kitty cat, he cried out, "What,
aughing at me? That makes me angry," he
houted. The Hare said, "It is true Master Lion,
ut I can tell you how to get a great big powerful
oice." Now, the Lion did not really believe the
iare. He knew that the hare was a trickster.
itill, the Lion ordered the hare to give him a
eally powerful voice.

The hare smiled slyly and advised the Lion. "[I]f
you want a strong voice, you must do exactl[y]
what I tell you to do--no matter how much [it]
hurts." Then the hare told the Lion what to d[o].
"Go deep into the forest, and find a bees nes[t]
with bees buzzing around and a honeycomb wit[h]
honey dripping down." "Then Master Lion," h[e]
said, "you must grab the nest and eat the bee[s]
nest, honeycomb, bees, and all." The hare tol[d]
the Lion that it would hurt quite a bit. He als[o]
told the Lion, "You must KEEP YOUR MOUT[H]
CLOSED while you chew. If you want a voic[e]
like big thunder," warned the Hare, "you mus[t]
keep your mouth closed!"

And so, the Lion went into the forest. There he
found a bees nest and honeycomb. He jumped
up and grabbed the bees nest with the bees
buzzing around, and a honeycomb with the honey
dripping down. He put them in his mouth and
began to chew. The bees started stinging him in
his esophagus, way down to his 'stomacus.' His
mouth was mingling, his tonsils were tingling,
and it hurt. The pain brought tears to his eyes.
He chewed and chewed, but he did not open his
mouth! He chewed and chewed, and he had to
clear his throat. "Grrr! GrrRR! GRRRR! A deep
sounding growl came from inside his throat. "Is

that my voice?" the Lion asked himself. He cleared his throat again. Once again, a growl came from deep in his throat. This time it was much louder! "That is my voice!" he shouted. Then the Lion opened his mouth wide and let out a great big roar! It was a GREAT BIG VOICE. "RRRRRROAR!"

"Is that thunder?" the animals of the forest asked "It sounds greater than thunder!" All of the animals came to see what this unusual noise was Simba, the Master Lion, stood proudly in front o his palace, and he let out another magnificen roar. This time the giant trees of the fores shook, mountains and hills quaked, and the animals were impressed! The Lion now had a big, big, big voice. And even to this day, it is one of the most awesome sounds in the forest anc plains of the motherland.

Sometimes you must go through some pain to ge what you want.

The StoryMan

THE LION AND THE WISEMEN
As told by Jamal Koram the StoryMan
A Story from Ethiopia

In days gone by, three wise men, who were very wise in some things, lived in an ancient kingdom of Africa. These men did nothing but read and study, experiment and think. They did not play basketball. They did not play music, nor did they sing songs. These wise men did important things like study astronomy, mathematics, physics, chemistry, psychology, and languages. They each spoke five different languages, but they never went out to mix with other people.

One day, the three men asked the council of elders, who ruled the kingdom, if they could travel anywhere they wished. The elders said "Yes," and so the three wise men began a journey to Zimbabwe. On the way there, the three wise men stumbled upon a Lion! Fortunately, for them, the Lion was dead. The first wise man said, "Let us bring this Lion back to life." The other two agreed, and each one offered to do something to bring the Lion back to life.

"I will put his bones to his skin," said the first man. "I will put air into his lungs," said the second man. "And I will put motion back into his limbs," said the third wise man.

As they talked, another traveler came by and overheard them. "Hodi, my brothers! I cannot believe what I am hearing. You are going to make the Lion live again?" Hearing this, the three men began shouting at the traveler. They told him that he was very foolish. "How could we be eaten by a Lion whom we have brought back to life? You are simple, go away!"

The traveler tried to argue with the decision to bring the Lion back, but it was no use. The wise men were determined. The traveler decided to stay, so he climbed into a tree and watched.

The wise men began their work. The first one put the Lion's bones to his skin. The second one put air back into his lungs. The third man put motion into the Lion's limbs.

Well now. Sure enough, the Lion came back to life, and he was very, very, very hungry! With a loud roar, he jumped on the wise men and ate them -- one, two, three. In a nearby tree, the wise traveler could do nothing but watch and be still. He waited until the Lion, his belly full, walked away. Then the traveler climbed down. As he jogged away, he said to himself, "Foolish is the person who cannot recognize good advice."

"You are never to wise to learn another thing."

The StoryMan

THE DONKEY IN THE LION'S SKIN: AN AESOP FABLE
As told by Jamal Koram the StoryMan

One day, a donkey found a Lion's skin, complet with head, tail, and claws. He put it over himsel and went into town to scare people. As soon a the townspeople saw him, they ran in fea because they thought that the donkey was really Lion. For a while he ran around scaring folks b pretending to be a Lion.

Pretty soon, he began to think that he WAS Lion! He saw Br'er Goat and thought. "I'll scar him with my mighty roar." The donkey opene up his mouth to roar and out came a very LOUL "HEE-HAW! HEE-HAW!" Br'er Goat jus looked. He sucked his teeth and said, "Shucks that ain't nobody but that jive old donkey. Ha me fooled 'til he opened his mouth."

Sometimes it is better to be yourself and to kee your mouth shut!

The StoryMai

WHEN LIONS COULD FLY
As told by Jamal Koram the StoryMan

Mr. Lion used to be able to fly. Oh yeah! Hi.
wings spread out about twenty feet wide, and no
one living thing was safe from his attacks. As a
matter of fact, Lion would kill animals for fooc
and pile the empty bones in his backyard. He
had two white crows guarding those bones
Everyday he reminded them that his bone.
should not be broken, "cause he didn't want no
broken bones."

Well now. One day, little Mainu the frog hearc
the Lion tell the crows not to let the bones be
broken. Mainu was curious about that, and when
the Lion left to go hunting, Mainu crept into hi
backyard. "Hey! You crows," yelled the frog
"What you doin' over there lookin' at then
bones!" The crows screeched back at Mainu
"Get away from here you little green thing you
We are the Lion's personal guards. Make track
Jack, and get on out of here!"

Now, Mainu did not like the way the crows hac
talked to him, and he decided to do them some

harm. After a few minutes of conversation, he convinced the crows to leave the bones and to let him watch over the bones. He told them that they hadn't had a break from watching those bones in such a long time, that now, while he was there, would be a good time to take time off. The crows quickly agreed and away they flew.

After they left, Mainu commenced to breaking them bones. Oh yeah! He had a good time. He broke this bone, and that bone, a left bone and a right bone. He went up one side of the Lion's backyard, and down the other side--breaking bones. Mainu had a bone-breaking good time! By the time the crows got back, ALL the bones in the Lion's backyard were broken. The crows looked at the bones and became very frightened. They were afraid of what the Lion would do when he returned. Mainu told them. "Don't worry. If the Lion wants me, he can find me at the pond."

Meanwhile, Lion was laying in the tall grass about to jump on an antelope. He spread his huge wings and got ready to fly, but he didn't move! No siree! He couldn't even flop those

things. "Umph!" "Arrgh!" "Ohhh!" "Something's happened to those bones," he thought. Angrily the Lion raced toward his house. When he arrived, he saw bone fragments all over his backyard.

Old Brother Lion could not believe his eyes. "What happened to the bones?" he roared. At first, the crows were filled with terror. They trembled as the Lion ranted and raved. Then they realized that the Lion wasn't flying, and so they began to mock the Lion. Oh yeah! Those white crows started snickering, flying around, and showing off something fierce. They were flapping their wings, doing loop-de-loops, and just having a good time. They sang out:

> *"When you left this morning*
> *you said, 'bye, bye'*
> *Come back this evening*
> *you can't even fly!"*

"Ha, Ha, Ha, Ha," they cried. Mainu, the frog down at the pond, broke all of your bones, silly Lion." The two crows just cracked up laughing. However, it was to be their last laugh for the Lion still had some powers. At that very moment, he made the crows mute.   They couldn't talk anymore.

The Lion ran to the pond. He spied Mainu sitting on a lily pad. He crouched down and tried to creep up on the little green frog. When he was just about to leap onto the frog, Mainu dove into the water and came up on the other side of the pond.   Lion tried to catch him again and again. But the more he tried, the quicker the frog jumped. It was no use. So, after a time, the Lion went back home to think about what he would do now that he could no longer fly.

From that day on, Lions have had to walk and run and creep up on their food.

Do not leave unloyal people to guard the things that you treasure. Use your strength and powers to help others--after you have helped yourself, your family, and your community.

The StoryMan

I hollered across the street, but nobody was home. This story is gone.

THE LION'S SEVEN FRIENDS
By Jamal Koram the StoryMan

In the forest, the Lion, Jumbe (joom-bay), chief of the city, had seven friends. These were friends he grew up with, and he loved them very much. Well, he really only loved six of them. The seventh friend, the Lion did not like so well. Whenever they would argue, the seventh friend would tell the Lion that she was worth more to him than all of his other friends put together. The Lion would always get angry, and the two would argue violently.

Well now. War came to the land, and because the Lion was the Jumbe, he had to go and fight. Early one day he began the journey to the battlefield. As he traveled, he thought about his friends. He wondered if any of them would mourn for him if he were killed while fighting. This thought made him more and more curious. He turned around and went back to the city. The Lion arrived in the city late that evening and went to the house of his first friend. He sang:

Old friend of the Lion [Jumbe]
Good friend of the Lion [Jumbe]
I bring you news of the Lion [Jumbe]
Sad, sad news of the Lion [Jumbe]

The friend answered, saying, "Who is it? What news do you bring? What has happened to the Lion?" The Lion pretended to be a frog, and he sang:

It is I, Mainu the frog [Jumbe]
The Lion died in the war [Jumbe]
The Lion died in the war [Jumbe]

When the friend heard that the Lion was dead, he shouted with glee. "Good! That is good for him. He was always mean and troublesome." The first friend said, "Now, I won't have to be bothered with him anymore." The Lion was surprised to hear these things from his favorite friend. He was very sad.

Walking slowly, the Lion went to the homes of each of the friends whom he loved very much. At each house his friends all sang the same song-- "Good, I'm glad he's gone! It only goes to prove that those who do wrong will always be punished," they said. Hearing these things from his so-called friends made the Lion very depressed. "Me can't believe it!" he cried.

Finally, the Lion reached the home of the seventh friend--the one he did not like so well. This was the friend with whom he always argued and fussed. "I don't know why I am coming to this house," thought the Lion. "If my good friends were glad that I am dead, I KNOW what this friend will say," Sadly, the Jumbe sang this song:

Old friend of the Lion [Jumbe]
Good friend of the Lion [Jumbe]
I bring you news of the Lion [Jumbe]
Sad, sad news of the Lion [Jumbe]

The friend answered, saying, "Who is it? What news do you bring? What has happened to the Lion?" The Lion pretended to be a frog, and he sang:

It is I, Mainu the frog [Jumbe]
The Lion died in the war [Jumbe]
The Lion died in the war [Jumbe]

This friend, that the Lion did not like so well, was so sorry, so sorry, so sorry to hear that her friend, the Lion was dead. She cried out loud:

My friend, my friend, my friend [Jumbe]
Let him live again [Jumbe]
Though he treats me bad, my friend [Jumbe]
Let him live again [Jumbe]

When he heard the loyalty of this friend, the Jumbe let out a mighty roar. "RRRRoarrrr!" Hearing this roar, the other so-called friends knew that the Lion lived. Gathering up a few possessions, they quickly left their homes, never to return. These six friends left because they knew that they had betrayed their leader. They left quickly because they had betrayed their friend.

Treat your friends well, in good times and in bad times, and never, never, never betray your friends.

The StoryMan

"I threw my shoe to close the door.
This story is done."

THE LION AND THE FOX: AN AESOP FABLE
As Told
By Jamal Koram the StoryMan

The Lion was getting old and feeble. His leg
were stiff, and his eyesight was poor. He coulc
no longer hunt for his food. Since he could no
hunt for his food, the Lion knew he would soor
die. And so, the old cat came up with a plan
"What I will do," he thought, "is to invite m
friends to my house. When they come in, I wil
eat them up!" This plan was good for the Lion
but no good for his friends.

One sunny day, Mister Antelope came by th
Lion's cave. The Lion called to him. "Oh Miste
Antelope!   Mister Antelope! Please come anc
visit with me!" The antelope agreed, asking th
Lion how he was feeling.   "My back hurts,
complained the Lion. "My knees hurt, and m
head hurts. Please come in and fix me some tea.
"O.K.," answered the antelope.   As he wa
preparing the tea, the Lion crept up on him.
Before the antelope realized what was

appening, the old Lion jumped on him and ate
im up.

wo days later, Br'er Lion heard his friend the
onkey up in the trees. "Mister Monkey! Mr
Ionkey! Please come down and visit with me."
).K.," said the monkey, "Hiya feeling?" "Oh Mr.
Ionkey, I'm not feeling too well. My back hurts,
y knees hurt, and my head hurts. Please come
 and read the daily newspaper to me." "O.K.,"
iswered the monkey.

s the monkey read the newspaper, the Lion
ept up on him. Before the monkey knew what
as happening, the Lion jumped on him and ate
m up.

iis unfair practice went on for days and days
id days. By and by, the fox came walking past
e Lion's cave. Br'er Lion called to him.
Iister Fox! Mister Fox! Please come and visit
e. I'm not feeling too well. I need you to come
d fix my bath water." Now, the fox was a wise
d cautious animal. Around the Lion's cave he
w many, many, many tracks and footprints
ing into the Lion's house, but he didn't see any

footprints coming out. "Excuse me, Brothe
Lion," said the fox, "I see where you had a lot of

visitors lately." "Oh, yes, yes," said the Lion, "n
friends love to come and visit me." "Well," sa:
the fox, "I've noticed that a lot of your frienc
have been going into your house, but not comir
out. When those friends come out," he said, "I
go in and fix you all the bath water you need
After saying that, the fox trotted away, leavir
the hungry Lion looking dumbfounded.

Sometimes you can use the experience of others t
learn valuable lessons.

It is wise to learn from other's mistakes.

The StoryM:

THE LION AND THE ASHIKO DRUM
by Jamal Koram the StoryMan
A Fable from South Carolina

Tsara came from a large family which lived in the village of Sahesis. Her family was very close and shared with one another in many ways. Loaat, her husband, came from the northland coast. He loved his wife very much.

When they were first married, Tsara and Loaat had much fun. Tsara was a dancer, and even though Loaat was a healer, he enjoyed drumming. He would drum on his Ashiko drum and Tsara would dance the dance of the Griot, the harvest dances, the praise dances, and the dance of love. Deep into the night Tsara and Loaat would dance and drum.

There came a time when the husband and wife moved to the country to farm and to raise the children they hoped to have. At first, the work kept them very busy. The dancing and drumming became much less, until finally, there was none. Well, there was no dancing, but late

nto the night you could hear the Ashiko drum
hat Loaat would always carry.

3y and by, Tsara became very lonely for her
amily, and she would visit them quite often.
oaat questioned her, "Why must you visit your
amily so much? There is a lot of work here, and
 cannot do it all by myself."

'sara would answer, "You are the one who
vanted to come out here. You are the one who
pent all of our savings to come out here to farm.
ind look at my front," she said, "do you see
:hildren coming from there?"

oaat would shake his head and tell her to go
head.

)ne day, Tsara told Loaat that she was going
1ome, and started off. "Tsara," he called, "be
:ure you take the Wasdi road. A ferocious Lion
1as been seen on the Alani road. Do you hear
ne?" he yelled. His wife called back, "I've been
1ome before!" But she really wasn't listening.

'he husband watched as she walked off. "I love
rou," he said to himself, "and I miss you. Will

we ever dance again?" he mused, looking at hi
Ashiko drum.

Loaat started back to work. After a short while
he had a funny feeling inside. "Something i
wrong," he thought. Quickly he dropped what h
was doing and headed for the Alani road wher
the Lion had been seen. With the speed of
cheetah, Loaat ran down the road until he cam
to a huge Baobab tree on a curve in the road.

As he rounded the tree, he caught his breath
There was Tsara, and in front of her was a hug
Lion about to leap on her! Without thinking
Loaat reached for his Ashiko drum and began t
play. He beat out the rhythms to the dance o
the hunter.

Boom baat. Boom baat. Boom baat baat Boon
baat.

Simba, the Lion, stopped in his tracks and turnec
toward the drummer. Loaat kept drumming.

Boom baat. Boom baat baat Boom baat.

The lion tilted his head, first to one side, then to the other side, as if he were moving to the drum beats.

Boom baat. Boom baat baat Boom baat.

The husband yelled, "Run Tsara!" "Kimbia!" "Don't look back!" The wife ran, and she did not look back.

Boom baat. Boom baat baat Boom baat. Loaat continued to play the drum. Then, the Lion lifted his left paw, and then his right paw, as if dancing to the drum rhythms. Loaat said, "I must find a way out of this. Simba seems to like the sound of the Ashiko drum." Loaat thought if he could step back around the Baobab tree, he had a good chance to get away.

Boom baat. Boom baat baat Boom baat.

He hit the Ashiko, and took three steps backward, thinking that he could ease away from the Lion. But the Lion followed the healer's movements. Simba was actually dancing to the rhythms of the drum!

Boom baat. Boom baat baat Boom baat.

"Maybe, if I move a little quicker, I will lose him,
thought Loaat. He took three long, quick stride
backward around the curve and was about to tur
and run when the Lion ran up just as close as h
was before.   Then, a most surprising thin
happened. The Lion spoke!

"Healer, why are you trying to escape me? D
you not know who I am?"

Loaat could not believe his ears, so he kept o
playing-louder and faster.

BOOM BAAT.   BOOM BAAT BAAT BOON
BAAT!

"Healer!" shouted the Lion, "I am your guardia
and your muse. I am here to protect you!"

The drumming stopped.

"But you were going to kill my wife!" cried Loaat

The Lion protested, "No, no, no," he said. "I was only talking to her." Cautiously, Loaat asked what they were talking about.

"About both of you," explained Simba. "There is no reason why the two of you cannot be happier together. You both love each other. You both care for each other."

The Lion continued to speak.

"You want the Tsara of yesterday," he explained, "but yesterday is gone. Look at your wife as she is today. Give her what she wants and needs. Concentrate on her. Have patience, and you will see that the crops will grow, the laughter will flow, the harvest will come, and there will be little dancers for your drum rhythms."

"He is right, my strong one," said a voice from behind the Baobab. It was Tsara. As she stepped from behind the tree, she said, "I do love and respect you. I want to make you happy, too."

The husband and wife hugged and kissed each other as sparks of love jumped from their eyes.

The Lion flicked his tail, and Loaat suddenly had an urge to play the Ashiko drum.

Boom Boom baat do baat.   Boom Boom Boom Baat do Baat.   Boom Boom Boom.   Baat do baat.

And there, under the wide limbs of the Baobab tree, the dancer, the healer, and the Lion danced the dance of peace.

Sometimes when we are afraid of the future, we cling to the past.

Change your mind, and you will change your life.

Most times, what we travel miles to see, is closer then we think.

The StoryMan

THE LION AND THE HYENA
As told by Jamal Koram the StoryMan

A Lion was lost in the forest. A traveling hyena found the cub and brought it home. He thought about eating it, but had a better idea. He decided to train the Lion cub so that it would work for him.

The young cub learned quickly. As soon as he was big enough, he began to hunt for the hyena and for the hyena's family. Mister Hyena would eat most of the meat and would give Lion the scraps. Whenever the Lion would begin to think about who he was, the hyena would punish him. By and by, the Lion stopped trying to find out who he was.

After coming from a hunt one day, the Lion was walking past the hyena's house. He overheard the hyena and his wife talking. The wife said, "Dear, wouldn't it be wise to give the Lion a more comfortable place to sleep and let him eat more than the banana diet you have put him on. He may get out of control."

"Do not fret so," said the hyena, "he is unde
control. Besides, he does not know that he is
Lion."

"Still," said his wife, "I would feel much safer i
you would treat him better."

Hearing this, the Lion became very angry anc
also very curious. He was angry because he now
understood how he was being treated. At the
same time, he was curious to know who and what
a Lion was. "Maybe," thought the Lion, "the
hyena never wanted to go past the Hyena Forest
because I would find out who I am."

The next day the Lion went hunting as usual.
And, as usual, the hyena reminded the Lion not
to go past the Hyena Forest. However, today the
Lion had other things on his mind. Instead of
traveling down the hunting path, he took the road
leading out of the Hyena Forest.

Back at the hyena house, Mister Hyena
wondered why the Lion did not take his hunting
bag with him. He decided to follow the cat to
see what he was up to.

After hours of walking, the Lion cautiously crept out of the forest.   In front of him was a wide grassy plain.   The sun was shining brightly on the high grass.   Across the field of grass, Lion saw a huge hairy-looking animal staring at him.   Its hair raised on his back, and it began running toward the Lion.   The young Lion didn't know what to do.   Should he run?   What was this animal going to do?   He decided to stand his ground.

Rushing up to the Lion, the animal looked magnificent.   His golden fur glistened in the sunshine.   He stopped in front of the Lion, showing his teeth and snapping his massive tail. "Peace my brother," said the animal in a gentle voice.   "Why don't you come on over and join us?"

The young Lion could not believe his ears. Talking with the animal, he discovered that he was a Lion too!   This was the happiest day of his life.   As he sat around listening and talking to the others, he learned of the story of a young cub who was lost in the forest.

"Maybe that story is about me," thought the Lion. Suddenly, he remembered the hyena. He became very angry as he remembered how badly he was treated by the hyenas. Roaring loudly, he took off toward the Hyena Forest. Some of the other young Lions rushed to follow him. They caught him before he reached the forest.

"Whoa, my brother," said one of the Lions. "Don't rush into revenge so quickly. The hyena is small but he is not powerless. Think for a minute. He kept you down so long because of your power." Then, another spoke.

"The hyena will serve your purposes better if he is alive. He will spread the word of your strength."

There, at the edge of the lush green forest, the young Lion thought very hard on what was said. Sitting there, he suddenly spied hyena footprints on the path. Immediately he knew that he had been followed by the hyena. The Lion jumped up. "You have given me wise advice my brothers," he shouted running toward the hyena's house. "But I will never allow an enemy to kill me twice." Hearing this, the other Lions joined him.

No animal is a slave until s/he stops seeking freedom.

The StoryMan

QUEEN LIONESS: AN AESOP FABLE
As told by Jamal Koram the StoryMan

All of the animals in the forest were arguing about who gave birth to the most children. The gnu and the topi, the cheetah and the elephant and many others were all claiming the most children.

"I had five children at one time," claimed one. "So," said another. "I give birth twice a year." As everyone was talking, the Lioness walked by with her cub. "Oh, look," said the giraffe. "There's Miss Lioness. And how many young ones do you give birth to?" she asked the Lioness.

At first, Queen Lioness walked past the other animals, but then she turned and with a slight smile she said, "Just one, but that one is a LION!"

Quality is better than Quantity
Let us raise our children like the Queens and
Kings they are...

The StoryMan

THE HAIR OF A LION
As told by Jamal Koram the StoryMan
A husband and wife tale

A woman was having problems with her husband
They lived in an East African village near Lake
Abaya.   Sometimes the husband, Tefte, would
stay away overnight.   He often was late coming
home from work, and when he did come home on
time, he and his wife would argue and fuss, argue
and fuss.   This was no good.   *A husband and a*
wife should be gentle with one another.   The
woman, Nefti, would get very angry with her
husband.   Whenever he did something wrong
she would insult him and call him names
Sometimes, he would hit her.   This was no good
A husband and a wife should be gentle with one
another.

Well now.   The woman knew that she and her
husband needed help.   She wanted a divorce
Nefti loved her husband, but she did not
understand why he did the things he did.   "Men
are so difficult to live with," she would say.   "I
need some space and time for myself."

One day, Nefti decided to see one of the elders of the community who was very wise about marriage matters. She asked him how she might get a divorce. Nefti complained, "Tefte never takes any time with me. He comes home late. I think he is seeing other women. He abuses me and does not seem to appreciate me anymore. It is time for us to part!"

The wise elder listened to the young woman. He said, "I understand your problem, but let us try to think of another way besides divorce." He looked at her thoughtfully and said, "There is a natural herb that can make your husband a changed man. It will cure him of all your complaints."

Nefti wanted to know where she could get the natural herb. She wanted it immediately! *She loved her husband, and she knew that he loved her. A husband and a wife should be gentle with one another.* "To get this herb won't be easy," said the elder. "To prepare a potion, I must have the single hair of a living Lion!"

Nefti hesitated. But *she loved her husband and she knew that he loved her. A husband and a wife should be gentle with one another.*   Confidently, she announced , "I will do it! I will

get the hair of a Lion." The elder knew then how much she loved her husband, Tefte. He told her that he Lion would come to the river to drink and what she must do at that time.

The following day, Nefti and her friend, Negasti, walked to the river with a leather bag full of fresh meat. They hid in the bushes by the river and waited for the Lion. When the Lion walked out of the forest to the river, Nefti became very afraid. She had never seen such a magnificent Lion. He was very long and very big! She hesitated. Filling up with courage, she flung the meat to Simba, the Lion. The huge Lion ate the meat and walked back to the forest.

Each day, Nefti and her friend went to the river. Each day, she would feed the Lion fresh meat. After many days, she came out of the bushes and began to get closer and closer to the Lion. She became fearless. She was determined to get the hair of the Lion, *for she loved her husband, and she knew he loved her, and a husband and a wife should be gentle with one another.*

And so, one day, weeks later, Nefti walked up to the Lion, and he ate from her hand! As he ate, Nefti carefully stroked his mane and plucked out a single hair. As soon as she got the single hair, Nefti quickly retreated. As fast as she could she ran to the wise elder's home. She pleaded with him to hurry and make the potion.

The elder looked at her in disbelief. He almost did not believe that Nefti had taken a hair from a Lion. He had to be sure. After Nefti told him how she had plucked the hair from the Lion's mane, the elder was convinced. "Now, I have some truth for you," he said. "There is no potion that I can make to change your husband. The potion that will cure your husband is the patience, courage, and love that you showed with the Lion. If you can treat a Lion like that, surely you can treat your husband in the same manner." The elder explained. "Treat your husband with care and patience. Tell him of his responsibilities. Show him support for what he does. Do not be angry with him. Love and share parts of your life with him, and he should share with you. Do this, and he will change. That is the potion." Nefti shook her head to say that she understood. She said, "Asante sana, Mzee. I will do what you say. It is good. It is right." And so, Nefti did just that.

By and by, matters *did* change between her and her husband. Tefte grew more loving and more patient than ever before. Together they continued to grow in love and respect for each other. This was good. *For a husband and a wife should be gentle with one another.* A husband and a wife should be as ONE.

I looked in the eyes of my father, and I saw tomorrow. Tutaonana!

The StoryMan